养子女的拥有

曾经,有两位从未谋面的女人,一位你不曾记得,另一位被你称做母亲,这两位女人塑造了你的生命。一位是你夜的星辰,另一位是你昼的阳光,一位给予你生命,一位引导你生存,一位使你需要爱,另一位将爱给予了你,一位赋予你性别,另一位赋予你姓名;一位赐予你天赋,另一位帮助你走向理想,一位给予你情感,一位为你擦干每一次流下的泪水,一位为你寻找那个她不能给予你的家园,另一位终获得了她梦寐以求的孩子。现在,你含着泪眼问我那个出生命凝聚出的疑问:哪一位女人造就了我,我亲爱的孩子,你是两位母亲共同的结晶,你来自于两种不同形式的同一个爱。

白下区少年宫 晓艳书

Motherbridge of Love

To all the children we love — M. B. L.
For Sophie and Sergeï, without whom the family would be incomplete! — J. M.

Barefoot Books
124 Walcot Street
Bath, BA1 5BG, UK

Barefoot Books
2067 Massachusetts Ave
Cambridge, MA 02140, USA

Text copyright © 2007 by Mother Bridge of Love. Illustrations copyright © 2007 by Josée Masse
The moral right of Mother Bridge of Love to be identified as the author and Josée Masse
to be identified as the illustrator of this work has been asserted

This book has been printed on 100% acid-free paper. Graphic design by Barefoot Books, Bath
Reproduction by Bright Arts, Singapore. Printed and bound in Singapore by Tien Wah Press Pte Ltd
This book was typeset in Present and Albertina MT Regular. The illustrations were prepared in acrylics on Strathmore paper
Hardback ISBN 978-1-84686-047-8

British Cataloguing-in-Publication Data: a catalogue record for this book is available from the British Library

1 3 5 7 9 8 6 4 2

Library of Congress Cataloging-in-Publication Data

Xinran, 1958-
Motherbridge of love / Xinran Xue ; [illustrated by] Josée Masse.
p. cm.
ISBN 978-1-84686-047-8 (alk. paper)
1. Motherhood--Juvenile poetry. 2. Adoptees--Poetry. 3. Mothers--Juvenile poetry.
4. Children's poetry, American. I. Masse, Josée, ill. II. Title.

PR6124.I57M68 2007
895.1'352--dc22

2006038846

Motherbridge
of Love

Text provided by Mother Bridge of Love

Illustrated by Josée Masse

Barefoot Books
Celebrating Art and Story

Once there were two women
who never knew each other.

One you do not know.
The other you call Mother.

Two different lives shaped to make you one.

One became your guiding star;
the other became your sun.

The first one gave you life;
the second taught you to live it.

The first gave you a need for love;
the second was there to give it.

One gave you a body, the other taught you games.

One gave you a talent. The other taught you aims.

One saw your first sweet smile;
the other dried your tears.

One found a home for you
that she could not provide.

The other prayed for a child;

her hope was not denied.

And now you ask, of course you do,
The question others ask me too:

This place or your birth place —
which are you a daughter of?

Both of them, my darling –

and two different kinds of love.

Source Note

The poem you have just read was submitted anonymously by an adoptive mother to the charity Mother Bridge of Love (MBL). The text at the front of the book presents the poem in simplified Chinese. Founded in 2004, MBL is a charity that reaches out to Chinese children all over the world, in order to develop a connection between China and the West, and between adoptive culture and birth culture. It has three missions: to promote cultural awareness and understanding between the East and the West; to bridge the gap between adoptive parents and the adopted Chinese children, helping the children find their cultural roots; and to provide educational and other forms of support to children living in poor rural areas of China.

Among its many objectives, MBL coordinates a travel initiative, which allows Chinese children who have grown up abroad to become more familiar with the real China — the countryside, where most of the adopted children were born. This initiative also gives adoptive parents a chance to learn more about their children's heritage.

To print your own keepsake of the
Chinese poem at the front of this book, please visit
www.barefootbooks.com

To learn more about
Mother Bridge of Love and its many
offerings, you can visit their website at:
www.motherbridge.org

Barefoot Books
Celebrating Art and Story

At Barefoot Books, we celebrate art and story that opens
the hearts and minds of children from all walks of life, inspiring
them to read deeper, search further, and explore their own creative gifts.
Taking our inspiration from many different cultures, we focus on themes that
encourage independence of spirit, enthusiasm for learning, and sharing of
the world's diversity. Interactive, playful and beautiful, our products
combine the best of the present with the best of the past to
educate our children as the caretakers of tomorrow.

Live Barefoot!
Join us at *www.barefootbooks.com*